This Walker book
belongs to:

RO

_____

_____

_____

B is for
Baby

Atinuke

Angela Brooksbank

WALKER BOOKS
AND SUBSIDIARIES
LONDON • BOSTON • SYDNEY • AUCKLAND

For Adia, with love! ~ A.

For my father also known as Baba, who took me to Africa when I was a Baby. ~ A.B.

First published 2019 by Walker Books Ltd, 87 Vauxhall Walk, London SE11 5HJ. ✪ This edition published 2020

Text © 2019 Atinuke ✪ Illustrations © 2019 Angela Brooksbank

British Library Cataloguing in Publication Data: a catalogue record for this book is available from the British Library ✪ ISBN 978-1-4063-9087-2 ✪ www.walker.co.uk ✪ 10 9 8 7 6 5 4 3 2 1

B is for
Baby.

B is for Beads.

B is for Basket.

B is for **Banana.**

B is for **Breakfast.**

B is for Brother.

B is for going to see **Baba.**

B is for **Bicycle.**

B is for **Bumpy.**

B is for Baobab.

B is for **Big.**

B is for **Butterfly**.
B is for **Bird**.

B is for **Beautiful.**

B is for **Baboon.**

B is for Bus.

B is for Bridge.

B is for
Bougainvillea.

B is for
Bungalow.

B is for ... Baba!

B is for ...

Bananas?

B is for ...
Baby!

B is for **Biscuit!**

B is for Biscuit, Bananas and Baba.

B is for Baboon,

B is for Bicycle, Brother and Basket. And...

Bungalow, Bridge and Bus.

Butterfly and Bird.

B is for
Baby.

Look out for:

Baby goes to Market

ATINUKE · ANGELA BROOKSBANK

978-1-4063-6516-0

A Charlotte Zolotow Award Honor Book

"A delightful book sure to appeal to mischievous babies and toddlers everywhere" BookTrust

A Children's Africana Awards Best Book for Young Children selection

A Mathical Award Winner

"This is brilliant ... beautiful" Candice Braithwaite, Make Motherhood Diverse

A New York Public Library 100 Best Books for Kids selection